THERE ARE CRIMES
AND CRIMES

. . . crimes of violence, crimes of treachery and intrigue, crimes of omission so cunningly calculated that they pass unperceived. Who is not guilty of one of them?

Alfredo Traps, a traveler in textiles, believes himself innocent—or at least no worse than the next man. Then, stranded one afternoon in a small village, he finds lodging with an eighty-year-old retired judge.

At dinner that night, the Judge entertains his ancient friends—one a former defense attorney, one a former prosecuting attorney, and the third a one-time executioner. It is their custom, while enjoying the rich food and choice wines, to restage famous trials. But, as Traps' host remarks, it is "most fun" when they are able to "play with living material."

This night, Alfredo Traps good naturedly offers to play the part of "defendant." And now the game begins, a mock trial pl___ ___ ___ h laughter and high s___ ___ the cross examinat___ ___ ___ ___ suddenly, for Trap___

Brilliant ___ ___ tour de force that ___ ___ ___ and as a grotesque para___ ___ ___ ___ morality of man.

by *Friedrich Duerrenmatt*

THE QUARRY

TRAPS

THE PLEDGE

THE VISIT

THE JUDGE AND HIS HANGMAN

TRAPS

FRIEDRICH DUERRENMATT

Translated from the German by
Richard and Clara Winston

Ballantine Books • New York

FIRST BALLANTINE EDITION
DECEMBER, 1962
SECOND PRINTING—MAY, 1965

BALLANTINE BOOKS, INC.
101 Fifth Avenue, New York 3, N. Y.

Traps

Are real stories still

possible, stories for writers? If the writer does not want to tell about himself, romanticize, poeticize, universalize his ego; if he feels no inclination to talk about his hopes and failures, no matter how truthfully, or of the ways he sleeps with women, as though truthfulness would trans-

*port all these matters into the realm of univer-
sality instead of—and this is far more apt to
happen—into the realm of medicine or psychology; if he does not want this, but prefers
to be discreetly self-effacing, to decently keep
personal matters to himself, to work the material before him like a sculptor his stone, shap-
ing and developing it, and hoping thereby to
gain something of the classicist's faculty of not
falling too readily into despair, for all that he
can scarcely close his eyes to the sheer idiocy
that crops up wherever he may look—if this is
his endeavor, then writing becomes a far more
difficult and lonely as well as a more senseless
occupation. A good grade in literary history
does not interest him—how many have not already received good grades? What botches have
not received their prizes?*

*Let us say that he takes this view, that the
demands of the day are more important to him
than himself. But here too he finds himself in a*

dilemma, and his wares are at a disadvantage in the market place. Life offers plenty of sheer entertainment: the movies in the evening, each edition of the daily newspaper its flights of imagination. But on all but the cheapest level a modicum of depth is demanded, self-revelation, good old true-to-lifeness; there is a call for higher values, for moral principles, useful mottoes; something has to be discarded or supported, now Christianity, now popular nihilism. In a word, what is wanted is Literature. But suppose the author more and more stubbornly refuses to produce this sort of thing. Suppose he is well aware that the foundation of his writing lies within himself—in his faith or doubts, in his consciousness or unconsciousness, the proportion of each varying from case to case; but suppose also that he feels most strongly that none of this really concerns the public, that it suffices if in what he writes, shapes, forms, he presents the surface invitingly, and

nothing more; that he works away at the sur-
face and nowhere else, for the present keeping
his mouth shut, neither commenting nor sound-
ing off. Having reached this conclusion, he will
falter, hesitate, become utterly perplexed. He
is almost bound to. The suspicion rises that
there is nothing more to tell; abdication is
seriously weighed; perhaps it is still possible
to turn a few graceful sentences, but otherwise
the only recourse seems to be a switch to bi-
ology in order to grapple intellectually at least
with the explosion of humanity, the advancing
billions, the incessantly fertile wombs; or to
physics, or astronomy, in order to render to
oneself an orderly accounting of the scaffold-
ing in which we are suspended. All the rest is
for the magazines, for Life, Match, Quick *and*
Sie und Er: *the president in an oxygen tent;*
Uncle Bulganin in his garden; the princess with
her dashing Air Force captain; film stars and

12

dollar faces, interchangeable, already out of fashion almost as soon as they are spoken of. Alongside that, everyone's everyday life, in my case West European—Swiss, to be more precise—bad weather and boom times, cares and anxieties, deep personal shocks, but all without any connection with the universe, with the course of events and the discourse of nonsense, with the unwinding of necessities. Destiny has fled the stage; the play goes on only to allow the chance for lurking in the wings, outside the realm of all valid dramaturgy; in the foreground illnesses, crises, all things have become accidents. Even war has come to be dependent upon whether electronic brains predict that it will pay off. But we happen to know that, given all the factors, no such result can ever be registered, assuming that the computers function; the mathematics of the situation can only add up to defeats. But woe betide us if *results should be falsified, if there is illicit tampering with the mechanical brains. Yet even this is less appalling than the possibility that a screw should loosen, a tape go awry, a relay respond wrongly: the world doomed by a short-circuit, by a broken switch. We are no longer threatened by God, by justice, by fate as in the Fifth Symphony, but by an automobile accident, a dam breaks as the result of faulty construction, the explosion of an atomic plant through the error of some absent-minded laboratory technician, a wrong setting on an incubator. Into this world of breakdowns we follow our road, bordered by signboards advertising Studebaker, Bally Shoes, ice cream, and the tombstones of accident victims, but along whose dusty edges we may also find a few possible stories, with humanity visible in a commonplace face, with hard luck haphazardly acquiring a universal validity, with justice*

*and the judiciary process displayed, and per-
haps even with grace manifesting itself, caught,
focused, and reflected by the monocle of a
drunken man.*

An accident too,

though a minor one: a simple breakdown. Alfredo Traps, to mention his name, connected with the textile industry, forty-five years of age, still far from stout, of likable exterior, adequate manners, though these somehow betrayed mechanical training, so that beneath the veneer the peddler, a certain underlying element of crudity, showed through—this fellow citizen of ours had just been sailing down one of the great highways of the country in his Studebaker, and had every reason to believe he would reach his home in a fairly large city within the hour, when his car gave out. Simply would not go. Helpless, the shining red automobile sat at the foot of a small hill over which the road wound. In the north a cumulus cloud had formed, and in the west the sun still stood high, shedding an afternoonish light. Traps smoked a cigarette and then made a phone call.

The garageman who finally arrived to tow the Studebaker away handed down the verdict that he could not repair the damage before the next morning; there was something wrong with the fuel line. Whether or not this was true could not be determined, nor was it advisable to try to determine it; we are as thoroughly at the mercy of garagemen as once we were of

17

robber knights and, in still earlier times, of local gods and demons.

Too lazy to take the half-hour walk to the nearest railroad station and then the rather complicated though short rail trip back home to his wife and four children, all boys, Traps decided to spend the night where he was. It was six o'clock in the evening, hot, close to the longest day of the year.

The garage was on the outskirts of a village, a pleasant place that straggled away toward wooded hills, with a hillock in its center on which stood church, parsonage, and an age-old oak with iron rings and props; everything was solid and clean; even the manure heaps in front of the farmhouses were carefully layered and neatly squared off. There were a small factory, too, and several taverns and country inns, one of which Traps had often heard praised.

But the rooms were all taken; there was a poultry raisers' meeting, and Traps was directed

to a large private house that sometimes took
transients. Traps hesitated. It was still possible
to return home by train, but on the other hand
he was tempted by the hope of a possible adventure, for sometimes there were girls in the
villages—as in Grosbiestringen recently—who
appreciated a traveler in textiles. And so, with
renewed spirits, he set out toward the house.
Bells clanged from the church. Cows were
making for their various barns, mooing. The
two-story country house stood in a sizable
garden, its walls a dazzling white, flat roof,
green shutters, the building half concealed by
shrubs, clipped beech, and evergreens. Toward
the street there were flowers, mainly roses, and
in the midst of them an aged little man wearing
a leather apron, possibly the master of the
house, was pruning and snipping.

Traps introduced himself and asked for
lodgings.

"What is it you do?" the old man asked. He

had come up to the garden gate, smoking a cigar, and was barely higher than the gate itself.

"I am in textiles."

The old man examined Traps closely, peering over small, rimless glasses in the manner of the farsighted. "Yes, certainly, you can stay here overnight."

Traps asked the price of the room.

He was not in the habit of charging, the old man replied; he was alone, his son having gone to the United States; he had a housekeeper, Mlle Simone, who took good care of him, and he enjoyed having a guest now and then.

The commercial traveler thanked him. He was touched by this offer of hospitality and felt called upon to say that in the country, evidently, the good old customs had not yet died out.

The garden gate was opened to him.

Traps looked around. Gravel paths, lawn,

large shaded areas interspersed with patches of sunlight.

When they reached the roses, the old man remarked that he was expecting several gentlemen for the evening. With great care he snipped away at a rosebush. Friends from the neighborhood were coming, he said; two of them lived in the village, one farther off toward the hills; they were retired like himself, attracted here by the mild climate and the absence of föhn wind; all were lonely, widowed, eager to know about anything new, stimulating, and lively; and so it would be a pleasure to him to invite Herr Traps for dinner and the little stag party that always followed.—

The commercial traveler was taken aback. He had intended eating in the village, at that well-known country inn. At the same time, he could not very well turn down the invitation. He felt obligated. After all, he had been offered a night's lodging gratis. He did not want to seem the typical discourteous urbanite. And so he pretended to be overjoyed. His host showed him up to the second floor. The room was pleasant, with running water, wide bed, table, comfortable chair, Hodler painting on the wall, old leather-bound volumes in the bookcase. Traps opened his valise, washed, shaved, patted himself with eau de cologne, walked over to the window, lit a cigarette. A great disk of sun was sliding down toward the hills, irradiating the beeches. He ran quickly over the day's business: the order from Roacher, Inc.—not bad; the difficulties with Wilholz—the fellow was asking for a five-per-cent discount, but he would really twist his neck for him! Then memories bobbed to the surface. Disordered commonplaces: a planned adultery at the Touring Hotel; the question of whether he should buy his youngest boy (his favorite child) a set of electric trains; the thought that he really ought to telephone his wife and let her know what was detaining him. But he did not take the trouble. It was an old story. She was used to it, and would not believe him anyhow. He yawned, allowed himself another cigarette. Watching through the window, he saw three old gentlemen come marching up the gravel path, two of them arm in arm, the third, a fat, bald-headed old fellow, bringing up the rear. Greetings, handshakes, embraces, words about roses.

Traps moved away from the window and examined the bookshelves. To judge by the titles, he was in for a dull evening. Hotzendorff: *Homicide and the Death Penalty;* Savigny: *System of Contemporary Roman Law;* Hölle: *Interrogation Practice.* The commercial traveler saw the whole situation. His host was a jurist, perhaps a former lawyer. He prepared himself mentally for an evening of boring discourse. After all, what did these educated blokes know about real life? Nothing—you know how the

law is. There was also the unpleasant possibility
that the talk would turn to art or such matters,
in which he might mildly make a fool of himself. Oh, well, if he were not in the thick of
the struggle for existence, if he were not in
business, he too would be able to keep up with
higher things.

And so he went downstairs without much
enthusiasm. The old parties had settled down
on the still sunlit veranda, while the housekeeper, a woman of robust proportions, was
setting the table in the adjoining dining room.
Traps was quite jolted when he saw the company more closely. It was fortunate that his
host gave him a chance to recover by coming
forward to greet him. The master of the house
was now dressed with almost dandyish care, his
sparse hair carefully brushed, but his frock
coat was much too big for him. He welcomed
Traps with a little speech that gave the commercial traveler some cue to his further con-

duct. Traps murmured that the pleasure was all on his side; playing the part of the worldly businessman, he bowed coolly and aloofly, and wistfully thought to himself that he had only stayed in this village in the hope of picking up some girl. That was out of the question now. He found himself confronting three more old codgers not a whit less queer than their ancient host. Like monstrous crows, their black-clad figures filled the summery veranda with its wicker chairs and gay awnings. Their frock coats were of the best material, as he immediately noted, yet the men looked slovenly, superannuated, untidy, except for the bald-headed fellow (Pilet by name, seventy-seven years old, as his host informed Traps in the course of the introductions that now began), who sat stiffly and primly upon an extremely uncomfortable stool even though there were several easy chairs available. Herr Pilet was, if anything, decked out with excessive formality,

25

had a white carnation in his buttonhole, and constantly stroked his black-dyed, bushy mustache; a man obviously retired on a pension, perhaps a former sexton or chimneysweep whom luck had raised to prosperity, perhaps even a railroad engineer. By contrast, the other two looked all the sloppier. One of them (Herr Kummer, eight-two) was even fatter than Pilet, simply enormous; he looked as though he were made of greasy sausages. He sat in a rocking chair, his face blowsy, sporting the swollen nose of an alcoholic, and jovial pop-eyes behind gold-rimmed pince-nez. He was wearing a nightshirt under his black suit—probably because he had forgotten to change it—and his pockets leaked newspapers. The other (Herr Zorn, eighty-six), lank and ca-daverous, had a monocle clamped into his left eye, dueling scars on his face, a hooked nose, a snow-white lion's mane, a sunken mouth—all in all, an antediluvian phenomenon with vest

26

buttoned awry, and socks of two different patterns.

"A drink?" the host asked.

"Yes, thank you," Traps replied, dropping into an armchair.

The lank, cadaverous fellow eyed him with interest through the monocle. "I trust Herr Traps will take part in our game?" he asked.

"Why, of course. I always like games."

The old parties smiled, rocking their heads.

"Our game is possibly a little strange," his host confessed cautiously. "What we do at these evenings is to play at our old professions."

The guests smiled again, politely, discreetly.

Traps was perplexed. How was he to interpret that?

"Well," his host explained, "I used to be a judge, Herr Zorn a prosecuting attorney, and Herr Kummer a trial lawyer. And we play at holding court."

"Ah, I see," Traps said. The idea struck him

as not bad. Perhaps the evening wasn't altogether lost after all.

His host regarded the commercial traveler solemnly. In general, he explained in a gentle voice, they did revivals of famous historical trials: the trial of Socrates, the trial of Jesus, the trial of Joan of Arc, the trial of Dreyfus. Recently they had held the Reichstag Fire trial, and once they had found Frederick the Great *non compos mentis.*

Traps was astonished. "Do you play this every evening?"

The judge nodded. But of course, he continued, it was most fun when they were able to play with living material, which frequently resulted in especially piquant situations. Only the day before yesterday, for example, they had had up before them a politician who had delivered an election speech in the village and missed the last train. He had been sentenced to

fourteen years in the penitentiary for extortion
and bribery.

"A tough court you have here," Traps declared with amusement.

The old men beamed. "A matter of principle
with us."

Then what part could he play in the game?
Traps asked.

More smiles, almost laughter.

They already had the judge, the prosecutor,
and the defense attorney, his host pointed out.
Moreover, these were posts that required
knowledge of the subject and of the rules of
the game. Only the post of defendant was un-
occupied—but he wanted to emphasize once
more that Herr Traps was under no obligation
to join in the game unless he wished to.

It happened that the idea appealed to the
commercial traveler. The evening was saved.
It was not going to be high-toned and boring;
on the contrary, it promised to be jolly. For

Traps was a simple fellow without any great mental powers or bent for thinking, a business-man, clever enough when he had to be, out for all he could get in his own line of work, but also fond of good food and drink, with a liking for crude practical jokes. He would be glad to play, he said, and would be honored to take over the vacant post of defendant.

"Bravo!" the prosecutor cawed, clapping his hands. "Bravo, there's a man speaking. I call that courage."

The commercial traveler asked curiously what crime would be attributed to him.

"An altogether minor matter," the prosecutor replied, polishing his monocle. "A crime can always be found."

All laughed.

Herr Kummer rose. "Come, Herr Traps," he said almost paternally. "We want to try the port this house has to offer. It's wonderful stuff. You must not miss it."

He led Traps into the dining room.

The big round table had been set most fes-
tively. The chairs were all high-backed; there
were dark pictures on the walls; everything
was solid and old-fashioned. From the veranda
came the chatter of the old parties; the sunset
shimmered through the open windows; birds
twittered outside; and on a smaller table stood
an array of bottles. There were more bottles
on the hearth, the Bordeaux in baskets.

The defense attorney poured carefully, with
somewhat tremulous hands, from an old bottle
of port. He filled two small glasses to the brim
and touched glasses with the commercial
traveler, but circumspectly, barely permitting
contact between the two glasses with their precious liquid.

Traps tasted the wine. "Excellent," he ap-
proved.

"I am your attorney for the defense, Herr
Traps," Herr Kummer said. "Therefore, let

the two of us drink to good friendship!"

"To good friendship!"

It would be best, the lawyer said, moving his red face with its alcoholic's nose and pince-nez closer to Traps, so that his huge belly, a soft, unpleasant mass, actually touched our friend—it would be best for the gentleman to confide his crime to him at once. If Traps would only do that, he could guarantee to bring him safely through the trial. The situation was not dangerous, of course, but its difficulties should not be underestimated, as the cadaverous prosecutor was still in full possession of his intellectual powers; he was someone to be feared, while the judge, their host, unfortunately inclined to strictness and possibly even to pedantry. These traits had worsened with age—the good man was eighty-seven, after all. In spite of all this, he, the defense attorney, had succeeded in saving most of his clients, or at least preserving them from the worst. Only in one case, that of a robbery accompanied by homicide, had he been unable to rescue his client. But it would be his guess that robbery with homicide was scarcely in Herr Traps's line. Or was it?

Unfortunately, he had committed no crime, Traps said, laughing. "Your health!" he said.

"Better confess it to me," his defense attorney said encouragingly. "There's no need for you to be ashamed. I know life; nothing surprises me any longer. Human destinies have filed before me, Herr Traps, frightful abysses have yawned before me—believe me!"

"Sorry." The commercial traveler grinned. "Really sorry, but here I stand, a defendant without a crime. Anyway, it's the prosecutor's business to find the crime—he said so himself, so let's take him at his word. A game's a game." He was curious to see what would come of it, Traps continued. "Would there be a real inter-rogation?"

"I should think so!"

"I'm looking forward to it."

The defending lawyer looked grave. "Do you feel yourself to be innocent, Herr Traps?"

The commercial traveler laughed. "Absolutely so." He thought the whole affair immensely amusing.

The defense attorney cleaned his pince-nez. "Mark my words, young friend, innocence doesn't matter one way or the other. Tactics are what count. It is sheer recklessness—to put it mildly—to feign innocence before our court. On the contrary, the most prudent thing is to accuse oneself of a crime right off. A good choice for businessmen, for example, is fraud. It may always turn out in the course of the trial that the defendant is exaggerating, that he really has not committed any actual fraud, but has only, say, suppressed a few facts, as is customary in business. The road from guilt to acquittal is difficult but not impossible. On the other hand, it is literally hopeless to try to maintain innocence, and the result is devastating. You will lose where you could win; moreover, the choice you are making forces you into a situation where you can no longer select your crime; you will have to have it imposed upon you."

Amused, the commercial traveler shrugged his shoulders. He was sorry he could not oblige, he said, but he could not think of a single misdeed that had ever brought him into conflict with the law.

The defense attorney replaced his pince-nez. He would be having his troubles with Traps, he remarked pensively; it would be tough sledding. "But, above all," he concluded, "consider every word you say; don't start blabbing, or you will suddenly find yourself condemned to years of penal servitude and nothing to be done about it."

The rest of the company came in. They sat down at the round table, made themselves comfortable, exchanged jests. First various entrees were served—cold cuts, deviled eggs, snails—and then turtle soup. All were in fine fettle; they spooned away contentedly, slurped without restraint.

"Well, defendant, what have you to offer us?" the prosecutor croaked. "A fine substantial murder, I hope."

The defense attorney protested: "My client is a defendant without a crime—a judicial rarity, as it were. He maintains he is innocent."

"Innocent?" the prosecutor exclaimed in astonishment. His dueling scars reddened, and his monocle slipped from his eye, almost falling into his plate, and swung back and forth at the end of its black cord.

The stunted little judge, who was breaking bread into his soup, paused, cast a reproachful look at Traps, and shook his head gravely. The bald, taciturn party with the white carnation likewise stared at him in astonishment.

The sudden silence was frightening. Not the

click of a fork or spoon, not a heavily drawn breath or sipping of soup could be heard. But at the back of the room Mlle Simone giggled softly.

The prosecutor recovered his composure at last. "We'll have to look into this," he said. "If a thing cannot be, it does not exist."

"Go to it," Traps laughed. "I am at your disposal."

Wine was served with the fish, a light, sparkling Neuchâtel.

"Well, then," the prosecutor said as he dissected his trout, "let us see. Married?"

"For eleven years."

"Children?"

"Four."

"Occupation?"

"I am in the textile industry."

"Ah, then you are a salesman, my dear Herr Traps?"

"Sales manager."

"Fine. And your car broke down?"

"As luck would have it. First time in a year."

"Aha. And before that?"

"Oh, in those days I still had my old car," Traps explained. "A '39 Citroën. But now I've got a Studebaker, red, a special job."

"An American car, eh? Well, well. Interesting. And acquired only recently, I take it? I suppose you were not a sales manager yet?"

"No, I was just a plain ordinary traveler in textiles."

The prosecutor nodded. "Boom times, eh?"

The defense attorney was seated beside Traps. "Watch your step," he whispered.

But the commercial traveler—or, rather, the sales manager, as we may now call him—proceeded without a care in the world to doctor his steak *tartare*. He had his private recipe: a few drops of lemon, a dash of cognac, paprika, and salt. Really, he declared happily, he had never enjoyed a pleasanter meal. He had always thought the meetings of the Utopia Club the best fun a fellow of his sort could ever hope for, but this evening was jollier by far.

"Ah," the prosecutor observed, "you are a member of the Utopia Club, then. May I ask what nickname they give you in the club?"

"Casanova."

"Wonderful!" the prosecutor bawled joyously, as though this information were of the greatest importance. He tucked the monocle back into its place. "We are all delighted to hear it. Does this nickname entitle us, my dear Traps, to draw any conclusions about your private life?"

"Careful," the defense attorney whispered.

"Within limits, my dear sir, within limits," Traps replied. "If I do have any extramarital experiences, it's a matter of pure chance. I don't make a point of it."

The judge refilled their glasses with Neuchâtel and took occasion to ask a question of his own. Would Traps have the kindness to give the assembled company a brief summary of his life? As they had decided to sit in judgment upon their dear guest and delightful miscreant, and perhaps to put him behind bars for years, it was only right that they should hear some of the more intimate details of his personal life. Affairs with women would be much to the point, of course, and let him not spare the salt and spice.

"Let's have it, let's have it!" the old gentlemen cackled in chorus. After all, they informed him, they had once had a procurer at their table who had favored them with a host of anecdotes of the most sensational kind concerning his business. Even so, they had sentenced him to only four years at hard labor.

"Now, now . . ." Traps joined in their laughter. "I haven't anything so colorful to offer. I lead a very ordinary life, gentlemen—

a life no different from anyone else's, I may just as well admit. Bottoms up!"

"Bottoms up!"

The sales manager raised his glass. With the utmost cordiality he met the birdlike eyes of the four old men, who gazed at him as if he were a particularly juicy morsel. Then they touched glasses.

Outside, the sun had set at last, and the infernal din of the birds had also subsided. But the countryside was still bathed in daylight; close by were the red roofs of the village, set among trees; farther off, the wooded hills; and in the distance the mountains, with glaciers still catching rays of sunlight: an atmosphere of sweet peace and rustic silence, a panorama of felicity, divine blessing, and cosmic harmony.

He had buffeted his way through a hard youth, Traps began while Mlle Simone changed their plates and placed a huge, steaming bowl of creamed mushrooms on the table. His father had been a factory worker, a proletarian led astray by the false doctrines of Marx and Engels, an embittered, joyless man who had never paid any attention to his only child. His mother had been a washerwoman, and had come to an early end. "I never went farther than grade school, no farther than grade school," he averred, tears in his eyes, torn between bitterness and deep sentimentality over his own meager lot.

They raised their glasses and toasted one another in Réserve des Maréchaux.

"Curious," the prosecutor said, "curious. No farther than grade school. You certainly have worked your way up in the world, haven't you?"

"I should think I have," Traps boasted, heated by the Maréchaux, inspired also by the jovial sociability of the occasion and the solemn beauty of the countryside outside the windows. "I should think I have. Only ten years ago I was nothing but a peddler, going from house to house with a little suitcase full of odds and ends. Hard work it was, tramping the roads, spending the night in haylofts and low-class inns. I started at the bottom in my trade, at the very bottom. And now, gentlemen, you ought to see my bank account. I don't want to brag, but does any one of you own a Studebaker?"

"Try to be cautious," his defense attorney whispered anxiously.

And what was his position now? the prosecutor inquired.

Again the defense attorney warned Traps to watch his step and not talk so much.

"Now—now I'm the sole agent for Hephaeston on the Continent," Traps announced, looking around him with an air of triumph. "Except for Spain and the Balkans—someone else has that territory."

The little judge heaped mushrooms on his plate. "I am familiar with the name Hephaestus," he said, chuckling. "A Greek god he was, and a great and subtle smith, who trapped the goddess of love and her lover, the god of war, in a net forged so fine as to be invisible. The other gods laughed till their sides ached to see the queer fish he had caught. But what Hephaeston may be, of which our friend has the honor to be sole agent, is a mystery wrapped in seven veils to me."

Traps guffawed. "You're on the right track, my dear host and judge. You said the key word yourself: veils. So there was this Greek god—I never heard of him before this moment—who wove a fine, invisible net. Well, you gentlemen of the court have no doubt heard of nylon, perlon, myrlon, and the other synthetics. Well, there is also Hephaeston, the greatest synthetic of them all. Transparent, tough as steel, equally useful in industry and in fashion, in wartime and peacetime. The perfect material for parachutes and, at the same time, the most delectable stuff for ladies' nightgowns, as I know from firsthand experience."

"Hear, hear!" the old men cackled. "Own experience—what do you know!"

Mlle Simone whisked away the plates again and brought in a roast loin of veal.

"A regular banquet!" the sales manager exclaimed with delight.

"I am pleased to see that you appreciate such delicacies," the prosecutor said. "And right you are. Our food is of the finest, and we enjoy quantity as well as quality. A menu that would have done honor to the last century, when people still had the courage to eat hearty. Let us praise Mademoiselle Simone! Let us praise our host, too—the little shrimp is a gourmet of the first water and does all the shopping himself. And as for the wines, they are provided by our friend Pilet, proprietor of the Bull and Stirrup in the next village. All praise to him, too. But now let us see how things stand with you, our virtuoso of the business world. We know something of your life now; it was a pleasure to be let into some of its secrets; and we are now fully briefed as to the nature of your occupation. There is only one minor point that has not yet been clarified: how in your professional life did you arrive at so lucrative a position? By sheer discipline and unflagging effort?"

"Be careful," the defense attorney whispered. "This is the danger point."

It had not by any means been easy, Traps replied, watching greedily as the judge began to carve the roast. First of all, he had had to undercut Gygax, and that had been a tough proposition.

"Ah, indeed. And who may Herr Gygax be?"

"My former boss."

"He had to be supplanted, you mean?"

"Got rid of, to give it to you straight from

46

the shoulder, the way we do in my line," Traps replied. He ladled gravy onto his meat. "You gentlemen won't mind if I speak frankly. It's dog eat dog in business, you know—an eye for an eye and a tooth for a tooth. If you try to handle people with kid gloves, you get kicked in the guts for your pains. I'm raking in the dough nowadays, but I slave like ten elephants for it, do four hundred miles a day in my Studebaker. I must admit I didn't exactly play fair when it came to cutting old Gygax's throat, but I had to get on. No help for it. Business is business, after all."

The prosecutor looked up from his veal with a gleam in his eye. "Get rid of, cut old Gygax's throat—those are pretty strong expressions, my dear Traps."

The sales manager laughed. "I mean them only as figures of speech, of course."

"And how is Herr Gygax these days?"

"He's dead—died last year."

"Are you crazy?" Trap's lawyer whispered to him. "You've gone clean out of your mind!"

"Last year," the prosecutor repeated sympathetically. "What a pity! How old was the man?"

"Fifty-two."

"So very young! And what did he die of?"

"Some disease or other."

"After you had taken his job?"

"Shortly before."

"Fine. For the present, that is all I need to know," the prosecutor said. "What luck, what luck we are having tonight! We've turned up a corpse, and that is the main thing, after all."

They all laughed. Even bald Pilet, who was reverently, pedantically devoting himself to his eating, refusing to be distracted from his pious occupation of devouring enormous quantities of food, looked up.

"Fine!" he said, stroking his black mustache. He said no more, and returned to his plate. The prosecutor solemnly raised his glass.

"Gentlemen," he declared, "in honor of this newest piece of data, let us imbibe the Pichon-Longueville 1933. A good Bordeaux to go with a good game."

They clinked glasses once more and drank to one another.

"Uhm!" Traps emptied his glass at one draft and held it out to the judge for refilling. "By God, that hits the spot."

Twilight had fallen, and the faces of the men at the table could scarcely be distinguished in the dusk. In the sky outside the window, the first shimmer of stars could be seen. The house-keeper applied a match to the candles in the three silver candelabra on the table, and the shadows of the assembled company danced on the walls like the wondrous chalice of some fantastic flower. A cosy intimacy, a warmth and fondness of each for all, spread through the company, accompanied by a relaxation of manners and a greater informality.

"Like a fairy tale!" Traps exclaimed.

The defense attorney raised his napkin to wipe the sweat from his brow. "You are the fairy tale, my dear Traps," he said. "I have never yet met a defendant who made such reckless statements with greater assurance."

Traps laughed. "Don't worry about a thing, my friend," he said. "Wait till the interrogation begins. I won't lose my head, I assure you."

This remark was followed by a deathly silence such as had fallen once before. All noise of chewing, of smacking lips, of sipping wine, ceased abruptly.

"You unfortunate wretch," the lawyer groaned. "What do you mean by 'wait till the interrogation begins'?"

"Oh," Traps said, heaping salad on his plate, "has it begun already?"

The old men grinned, looked slyly down at their plates, and at last burst into bleats of glee. The silent, equable, bald-headed man snig-

50

gered: "He didn't catch on, he didn't catch on."

Astonished, Traps paused in his eating. For a moment the roguish merriment of these dignified old men struck him as sinister. But the impression quickly passed, and he joined in their laughter.

"I beg your pardon, gentlemen," he said. "I thought of the interrogation as being more solemn, dignified, and formal, more like a regular court."

"My dear Traps," the judge explained, "the expression on your face is priceless. I see that our way of holding court strikes you as peculiar and much too gay. But, my dear fellow, the four of us here at this table are in retirement, which means that we are free from the needless red tape of forms and stenographic minutes and documents and statute books which is the burden of our ordinary courts. We dispense justice without regard for weighty tomes and Article This and Article That."

"Courageous," Traps replied, his tongue already beginning to labor for words, "courageous. Gen'lemen, I'm impressed. A court of law without the lawbooks—there's a smart new idea for you."

The defense attorney swayed heavily to his feet. He was going to catch a breath of air, he announced. Before they began on the fowl and the rest, it was time for a short stroll and a cigarette. Would Herr Traps care to accompany him?

They stepped down from the veranda into a warm, majestic night, for full darkness had descended. Golden beams of light extended from the windows of the dining room as far as the rose beds. The sky was bright with stars, but there was no moon, so that the trees stood out only as masses of denser darkness. One could barely make out the gravel paths down which they moved. The two men were clutching each other's arms. Both were heavy with wine; they staggered and reeled now and again, though they strove to walk straight. They smoked cigarettes, which made red dots of light in the darkness.

Traps took a deep breath. "God, what fun we're having in there," he said, gesturing toward the illuminated window in which loomed the sturdy silhouette of the housekeeper. "It's grand, grand."

"My dear friend," the defense attorney said, swaying and leaning on Traps to steady himself, "before we return and attack our capon, let me say a word to you in all seriousness and beg that you take what I say to heart. I like you, young man; I feel a tender affection for you, and I want to talk to you like a father. We are well on the way to losing our case right down the line!"

"That's too bad," Traps replied, guiding his lawyer cautiously along the gravel path and around the black pyramid of a shrub. They

came to a pool, divined rather than saw a stone
bench, and sat down. Stars glittered in the
water, and coolness wafted into their faces.
From the village came the sounds of an accordion, singing, and then the melancholy blast
of an alpenhorn. The Poultry Raisers' Associa-
tion was celebrating.

"You must pull yourself together," the lawyer
continued. "The enemy have already taken
vital bastions. The death of Gygax—there was
no need for that fact to have turned up at all if
you hadn't let your tongue run away with you
—the death of Gygax is a tremendous threat.
The situation is so bad that an ordinary lawyer
would have to throw in the sponge. But if I
stick to it and exploit all opportunities, and, above
all, if *you* exercise maximum prudence and self-
discipline, I can still save something from the
wreckage."

Traps laughed. This was an absolutely first-
class parlor game, he declared; he would make a

point of introducing it at the Utopia Club's next meeting.

"Isn't it, though?" the lawyer agreed, intensely gratified. "Brings a man to life again. My dear friend, I was dying by inches after I retired and was supposed to enjoy my old age here in this village without anything to do, without practicing my profession. Do you think anything ever happens here? Nothing at all, except that there is no föhn to give you headaches—that's all. What's the good of a fine climate? It's ridiculous, if the brain has no occupation. The prosecutor was practically on his deathbed; our host was thought to have cancer of the stomach; Pilet was suffering from diabetes; and I was having all kinds of trouble with my blood pressure. That was what came of our retirement. A dog's life. Now and then we met mournfully, talked nostalgically about our old professions and the successes we had had—that was our sole and rare pleasure. Then the prosecutor invented the game. The judge provided the house, and I placed my resources at the disposal of the company—after all, I'm a bachelor, and when you've been a lawyer for the upper crust all your life, you put aside a tidy little sum, my friend. You can't imagine how generous the robber barons can be when their defense attorney has won them an acquittal—lavish, I assure you. And the game has become our fountain of youth. Hormones, stomachs, gastric juices—everything is in balance again. Our boredom vanished; our energy, youthfulness, elasticity, and appetites were totally restored. Look at this. . . ." And, in spite of his paunch, he performed what Traps in the darkness vaguely recognized as gymnastic exercises. "We play our game with the judge's guests," the lawyer continued. "They function as defendants." He sat down again. "Sometimes we have salesmen, sometimes vacationers. Two months ago we had the privilege of sentencing a German general to twenty years at hard labor. He was passing through here on a walking tour with his wife. Only my skill saved him from the gallows."

"Marvelous," Traps exclaimed. "What a show! But you must be exaggerating a little when you speak of the gallows. After all, capital punishment has been abolished in Switzerland."

"In the official judicial system, yes," the lawyer corrected him, "but we are dispensing our own private brand of justice here, and we have reinstated it. It is precisely the risk of the death penalty that makes our game so exciting and so unique."

"And I suppose you have an executioner, too?" Traps said, laughing.

"Of course," the lawyer declared proudly. "We certainly do. Pilet."

"Pilet?"

"Ha, that surprises you, doesn't it?"

Traps swallowed hard several times. "But he is the proprietor of the Bull and Stirrup and provides the wines we have been drinking."

The lawyer smirked complacently. "He always has run a tavern. His work for the state was just a side line. Almost an honorary office. In his native Germany he was considered one of the most talented men in his profession. He's been with us for twenty years now, more or less in retirement, but he still keeps up to date in his craft."

A car passed on the highway, and the glare of its headlights irradiated the smoke of their cigarettes. For a second Traps caught a glimpse of his lawyer, a shapeless figure in a stained frock coat, with a fat, smug, jovial face. Traps shivered. Beads of cold sweat broke out on his brow.

"Pilet!"

"Why, what is the matter with you all of a sudden, my friend? I can feel you trembling.

Don't you feel well?"

"I don't know," Traps whispered, breathing heavily, "I don't know."

The image of the bald man leaped into his mind—how Pilet had sat at table dumb and unassuming, shoveling in his food; it was something of an imposition being asked to dine with a fellow like that. But, then, the poor fellow wasn't to blame for his occupation. The warmth of the summer night and the greater warmth of the wine tempered Traps's momentary outrage, inclined him toward feelings of tolerance, of being above prejudice. After all, he was a man who had seen a good deal, a man who knew the world, a big wheel in the textile industry, not some timorous, strait-laced, small-minded prig. In fact, on second thought, the evening would have been much the poorer without the executioner, far less piquant altogether. What a story this would make when next he saw the boys at the Utopia Club. The club might even invite the executioner someday to give a short talk to the membership; he would surely come in return for a small fee and expenses.

Having thus come to terms with his emotions, Traps laughed heartily. "That was a bombshell! Gave me quite a turn for a minute. The more I hear about this game, the funnier it gets."

"A confidence for a confidence," the lawyer said. They rose and, arm in arm, blinded by the light from the windows, fumbled their way back toward the house. "How did you do away with Gygax?"

"What makes you think I did away with him?"

"He's dead, isn't he?"

"But I had nothing to do with that!"

The lawyer stood still. "My dear young friend," he replied sympathetically, "I quite understand your hesitancy. Murder is the most painful of all crimes to confess. The defendant is ashamed, does not want to recognize his act, forgets it, represses it, drives it from his memory. He becomes touchy about the past altogether, burdens himself with exaggerated guilt feelings, and refuses to trust anyone, even his friend who is like a father to him, his defense attorney. And that, of course, is as wrongheaded as anything could be, for a real defense attorney loves murder; he is absolutely in seventh heaven if a murder is brought to him. Let's have it, Traps, my boy. I don't really begin to enjoy things until I face a tough problem, like an alpinist before a good ten-thousand-foot ascent. I speak as a regular old mountaineer myself. Give me a tough problem and my brain begins to function, to hum and purr; it's a joy to feel how smoothly it operates. For that reason, your distrust of me is your great mistake. Yes, your decisive mistake. So let's have your confession, old boy!"

"But I don't have anything to confess," the sales manager asserted.

The lawyer stared in astonishment. He gaped at Traps, the planes of his shattered old face grotesquely lit by the light from the window, through which came the clink of glasses and the ancients' gales of mirth.

"My boy, my boy," he growled reproachfully, "what are you up to now? After all I've said, do you still insist on these foolish tactics of yours? Are you determined to go on playing the innocent? Haven't you caught on yet? You have to confess, whether you want to or not, and there always is something to confess—that should have dawned on you by now. So let's get at it, my friend. Let's have done with all this coyness. Give it to me straight from the shoulder: how did you kill Gygax? In a sudden rage, wasn't it? In that case, we would have to be prepared for a manslaughter indictment. I'll bet the prosecutor is steering that way. I just have a feeling about that—I know the old boy."

Traps shook his head. "My dear, devoted defense attorney," he said, "the particular beauty of this game of ours—if I may be allowed to give my opinion, though this is the first time I've played it—is the way it gets under your skin and gives you the shivers. The game threatens to flip over into reality. All of a sudden you ask yourself whether you may not be a criminal after all, whether you did or didn't kill old Gygax. All your talk has been making my brain reel. And so, confidence for confidence. I am not guilty of the old bastard's death. Really not."

With that, they re-entered the dining room, where the capon had already been brought to the table and a Château Pavie 1921 was sparkling in the glasses.

Traps, overflowing with humor, went over to the grave, taciturn bald fellow and pressed his hand. The lawyer had explained about his former profession, he said, and he wanted to state that he, personally, could imagine no greater pleasure than to have so fine and up-standing a man to dine with. He, Traps, had no prejudices about that sort of thing—quite the contrary.

Pilet, stroking his dyed mustache, flushed and then murmured, with embarrassment: "De-lighted, delighted, will do my best."

After this moving exchange of civilities, the capon tasted all the better. The recipe was a secret of Mlle Simone's, the judge announced. They smacked their lips, ate with their fingers, extolled the masterpiece, drank their wine, toasted one another's health, and while they regaled themselves the trial took its course. The prosecutor, a napkin tied under his chin, hold-ing the drumstick to his masticating grease-smeared mouth, expressed the hope that the company would have a confession served up along with the fowl. "Surely, my dearest, my most honorable defendant," he probed, "surely you poisoned Gygax."

"No," Traps laughed. "Nothing of the sort."

"Then shall we say you shot him?"

"Not that either."

"Arranged an automobile accident?"

Everyone laughed except the defense attorney, who whispered sharply once more: "Watch out, this is a trap."

"Sorry, Friend Prosecutor, sorry," Traps cried exuberantly, "but Gygax died of a heart attack. And it was not even his first. He'd had one years ago and was supposed to be careful. He let on that he was fit as a fiddle, but there was always danger that any excitement would bring it on again. I know that for certain."

"Indeed? Who told you?"

"His wife."

"For heaven's sake, watch your step," the lawyer urged in his usual audible whisper.

The Château Pavie 1921 surpassed all expectations. Traps was already on his fourth glass, and Mlle Simone had placed an extra bottle near him. Raising his glass to toast the old gentlemen, the sales manager declared that, believe it or not, he had nothing to conceal. Just to prove this to the court, and no matter how unorthodox it seemed, he intended to tell them the truth, the whole truth, and nothing but the truth, despite the fact that his defense attorney had repeatedly urged him to be careful. The fact was, he'd had a little romance with Frau Gygax. The old bastard was often away on trips, after all, and had cruelly neglected the little woman, who was a mighty juicy piece. And so he, Traps, had undertaken to console her now and then, first on the couch in Gygax's living room and later on, as he grew more at home, in the Gygax marital bed. Things like that happened, after all; it was the way of the world.

At these words the old gentlemen froze for a moment in utter astonishment. But an instant later they screeched with pleasure. Bald-headed old Pilet, who said so little, tossed his white carnation into the air, crying: "A confession, a confession!"

The defense attorney alone did not share their glee. He pounded his fists despairingly against his temples. "Such folly, such folly!" he cried. His client had lost his mind, he protested. They must on no account believe his fabrications.

Indignantly, amid renewed applause from the rest of the company, Traps took issue with this. On the contrary, he knew exactly what he was saying. He was simply being frank. There began a long dispute between the lawyer and the prosecutor, a stubborn argument, half in jest, half serious, which Traps could hardly understand. It all hinged on the word *dolus*, and the sales manager did not know what the word meant.

The discussion grew steadily louder, more

violent, and more incomprehensible. The judge intervened and likewise became heated.

At the start Traps had made an effort to listen, trying to piece together the substance of the dispute, but his attention soon wandered. He breathed a sigh of relief when the housekeeper served cheese, Camembert, Brie, Emmentaler, Gruyère, Tête de Moine, Vacherin, Limburger, Gorgonzola. Turning his attention to these comestibles, Traps let *dolus* be *dolus*, but drank a glass to the bald man, who alone abstained from the discussion, which seemed to be above his head.

At last, however, the prosecutor turned to Traps again, his leonine mane in disarray, his face flushed, his left hand toying with the monocle. "Herr Traps," he asked, "are you still on friendly terms with Frau Gygax?"

All of them stared at Traps, who had thrust a piece of white bread spread with Camembert into his mouth and was chewing happily.

Before making his reply, he took another long swallow of Château Pavie. A clock was ticking somewhere, and from the village there came once more the distant sounds of an accordion and a male chorus.

He had kept away from there since Gygax's death, Traps explained. After all, he did not want to be responsible for compromising the reputation of a widow.

To his amazement, his explanation was the signal for another bout of fantastic, incomprehensible merriment. Everyone shouted with glee, and the prosecutor shouted. *"Dolo malo, dolo malo!"* He bellowed verse in Greek and Latin and hurled quotations from Schiller and Goethe, while the midget judge blew out all the candles except one. Bleating, hissing, and growling a wild accompaniment, he held his hands behind the flame of this single candle and deftly threw a shadow play upon the wall: he crooked his fingers this way and that to make goats, bats, devils, goblins, while Pilet drummed on the table until the dishes and glasses danced, chanting: "We'll have a death sentence, we'll have a death sentence."

The defense attorney alone held aloof from the general uproar. He pushed the platter of cheese in front of Traps. "Take some," he urged. "We may as well eat hearty. There's nothing left for us to do."

A Château Margaux was brought in, and the dusty bottle, vintage of 1914, restored quiet. Everyone gazed respectfully at the judge as he cautiously and with great deliberation began removing the cork, employing a curious, old-fashioned corkscrew that enabled him to draw the cork from the bottle as it lay on its side in the little basket. They watched in breathless suspense, for the cork had to be removed with the least possible damage, as it was the only proof of the age of the wine. (After four decades there was little left of the label.) The cork did not come out quite whole, and the remainder had to be scraped out with delicate care. But enough of the cork was left for the date to be legible. It was handed around the table, sniffed, admired, and finally solemnly presented to the sales manager as a memento, the judge said, of their wonderful evening. The judge now tasted the wine, licked his lips, and filled the other glasses. The rest of the company smelled the wine, sipped it, burst into cries of ecstasy and praise. The cheese was handed around again, and the judge requested the prosecutor to make his little speech and present the "case for the prosecution."

The prosecutor asked for new candles first, to mark the solemnity of the occasion. The task before him called, he said, for utmost concentration, for reverence and even composure.

Mlle Simone brought the candles and, amid tense silence, lit them. The sales manager felt that the atmosphere was slightly sinister, and a chill ran through him; still and all, he thought this a first-class adventure. Not for anything in the world would he have missed it.

Of all the company, only his lawyer seemed somewhat disgruntled. "Good, Traps," he said, "let us listen to the prosecutor's charge. You will be stunned to see what you have done with your careless tongue, what a mess you have made with your ill-advised tactics. If the situation was bad before, it is catastrophic now. But keep up your courage and I'll get you out of this predicament. Only don't lose your head; you'll need all your wits about you to come through with a whole skin."

The moment had come. There was a general clearing of throats. Someone coughed. Once more they toasted one another. And then, amid grins and chuckles, the prosecutor began his address.

"The greatest pleasure of our soiree," he said, raising his glass but remaining seated, "and its

crowning achievement, is that we have un-
covered a murder so subtly arranged that, of
course, it has brilliantly escaped the attention of
official justice."

Startled, Traps gave way to a momentary
outburst of annoyance. "Do you mean to say
that I have committed a murder?" he spluttered.
"Now, look here, that is going too far. My own
lawyer has already taken that crazy idea into
his head, and . . ." But then he remembered that
it was all in the game and began to laugh wildly,
uncontrollably. Ah, of course, what a wonderful joke! Now he understood it: they wanted
to talk him into believing he had committed a
crime. Terrific, absolutely terrific.

The prosecutor, regarding Traps with a dignified air, wiped his monocle and replaced it in
his eye.

"The defendant," he said, "doubts his own
guilt. A human impulse. Who among us knows
himself, who knows his own crimes and secret

misdeeds? However, I should like to lay stress upon one thing now, before the passions of our game rise once more to high tide. If Traps is a murderer, as I maintain, as I hope with all my heart, we are about to enter upon an hour of gravest solemnity. And rightly so. For the discovery of a murder is a joyful event, an event that makes our hearts beat higher, that confronts us with new tasks, decisions, duties. Therefore, before all else, I wish to congratulate our dear presumptive culprit, for without a culprit it is scarcely possible to discover a murder, to make justice prevail. A special health to him, then—to our friend, our modest Alfredo Traps, whom a kindly destiny has brought into our midst!"

Shouts of joy greeted this speech. All rose and drank to the sales manager's health.

Tears in his eyes, Traps thanked them and assured them that this was the most enjoyable evening he had ever spent.

The prosecutor too had tears in his eyes as he spoke again. "His most enjoyable evening, our noble friend tells us. Glorious words, gentlemen, deeply moving words. Let us recall the times when we performed our gloomy duties in the interest of the state. Then a defendant stood before us not as a friend, but as a foe. We had to thrust him away from us, whereas now we can take him to our hearts. To my heart, then!" Quitting his place, he threw his arms around Traps and hugged him tempestuously.

"Prosecutor, my dear, dear friend," the sales manager stammered.

"Defendant, my dear, dear Traps," the prosecutor sobbed. "Let us drop these formalities. My name is Kurt. To your health, Alfredo!"

"To your health, Kurt!"

They embraced, hugged, patted each other on the back, drank to each other; a tide of emotion washed over them, the joy that accompanies the blossoming of a new friendship.

"How everything has changed!" the prosecutor rejoiced. "Where once we were harried from case to case, from crime to crime, from verdict to verdict, now we have all the leisure in the world to build our case, to discuss, refute, dispute; we can speak and reply gaily and gladly, come to appreciate the defendant, to love him, to feel the warmth of his sympathy. Both sides are united in bonds of brotherly love. And, once that has come into being, crime has no weight, verdict no sting. Let me, then, express my appreciation for the murder which has been committed."

"Prove it, Kurt, my boy, prove it," Traps threw in, once again bathed in good humor.

"And rightly so, for we are dealing here with a beautiful, a perfect murder. Now, our delightful culprit may imagine that I am using such a term in a spirit of brash cynicism. But far from it; rather, I must characterize his deed as 'beautiful' in two respects: philosophically, and by reason of its technical skill. Let me assure you, my dear Alfredo, that our company has long since abandoned the narrow and prejudiced point of view that sees crime as ugly and terrible, and justice, on the other hand, as a thing of beauty. If we are to compare the two, I might say that justice can be the more terrible. But the duality is only apparent: the beauty of crime is indispensable for the beauty of justice; without crime we would have no justice. So much for the philosophical side. Let us now turn to an appreciation of the technical beauty of the act. I believe that appreciation is exactly the right word, for my address for the prosecution is not intended as a terrifying indictment that might embarrass and bewilder our friend, but as an appreciation that will reveal his crime for him, help it to flower, implant it in his consciousness. For the flawless monument of justice can be erected only upon the stainless pedestal of understanding."

The eighty-six-year-old prosecutor paused in exhaustion. In spite of his age, he had spoken in a loud voice and with sweeping gestures, eating and drinking a great deal all the while. Now he used the greasy napkin tied around his collar to wipe the sweat from his forehead and dry his wrinkled neck.

Traps was touched. He sat heavily in his chair, sluggish from the meal. He was satiated, but he did not want to be outdone by the four graybeards, although he had to admit to himself that he was hard put to match the vast appetite and vaster thirst of these old men. He was a hearty eater himself, but never in his life had he encountered such avidity as theirs. He sat gaping lazily across the table, flattered by the effusiveness of the prosecutor and listening as the bell in the church tower solemnly struck twelve, and then, rumbling in the distance, came the nocturnal chorus of the Poultry Growers singing: "Our life is like a voyage. . . ."

"Like a fairy tale," the sales manager exclaimed again and again, "like a fairy tale." And then: "So I'm supposed to have committed a murder. Me of all people? Would you kindly tell me how I did it?"

Meanwhile the judge had uncorked another bottle of Château Margaux 1914. The prosecutor, refreshed, began again.

"Now, what has happened?" he said. "How did I discover that our dear friend could justly boast of a murder? And not an ordinary murder —far from it. A masterpiece of a murder, committed without bloodshed, without resort to poison, guns, or anything so crude." He cleared his throat.

Traps, mouth full of cheese, regarded him in fascination.

It was in the nature of his profession, the prosecutor continued, to cherish the assumption that a crime might lurk behind every event, back of every person. The first indication that

friend Alfredo was one of those favored by
destiny, singled out for crime, lay in the cir-
cumstance that the commercial traveler had
driven an old Citroën only a year ago, and now
sat proudly at the tiller of a brand-new special-
model Studebaker.

"Now, I know," he continued, "that we live
in boom times, and so that detail could not be
taken by itself as prima-facie evidence of anything. It served merely as a clue, feeding the
premonition that we were on the verge of a
joyous experience—of the discovery of a murder, that is. That our dear friend assumed his
superior's former position, that he had to force
this superior out, and that the superior subse-
quently departed this life—all these facts were
still not proof, were merely elements confirming
my premonition, lending substance to it. Real
suspicion, founded upon a logical basis, did not
arise until we learned how it was that this
superior departed this life. From a heart attack.

At this point we had to apply all our skill, utilize all our keenness and subtlety, put two and two together, advance discreetly, creep up on the truth, recognize the extraordinary in the commonplace, certainty in uncertainties, outlines in the mist, to believe in a murder precisely because murder seemed ruled out.

"Let us consider the evidence at hand. Let us sketch a picture of the dead man. We know little about him; for what we know we are indebted entirely to our dear friend and guest. Herr Gygax was the sales manager for the company producing Hephaeston, a synthetic textile that we willingly believe possesses all the excellent qualities our dearest Alfredo ascribes to it. Gygax was a man, we may deduce, who was out for all he could get, who ruthlessly exploited his subordinates, who was adept at closing deals, although the methods he used were often more than questionable."

"Right you are," Traps cried enthusiastically.

"The old crook—you've got him perfectly."

"We may further conclude," the prosecutor continued, "that outwardly he played the part of a vigorous, robust man, a hard-hitting successful businessman bristling with good health, able to cope with any situation, a man who knew his way around. In order to maintain this image, Gygax carefully concealed the fact of his severe heart disease—here too we are quoting Alfredo. We may assume that he took the fact of his illness with a kind of defiant fury, as though it meant an admission of some kind of failure."

"Wonderful!" Traps exclaimed. It was simply uncanny; he would bet that Kurt had known the dead man personally.

"Be still, be still!" the defense attorney whispered sharply.

"But let us complete our portrait of Gygax," the prosecutor continued. "There is the additional fact that the deceased neglected his wife, whom we are to imagine as a mighty juicy piece

—at least, that is how our friend has described her. To Gygax only success counted, only business, externals, the façade, and it is safe to guess that he took his wife's fidelity for granted, in so far as he fancied himself far too extraordinary, too overpowering a man, for the thought of adultery ever to occur to his wife. For which reason it would have been a hard blow to him if he had learned of his wife's amusing herself with our Casanova of the Utopia Club."

All laughed uproariously. Traps slapped his thighs. He beamed all over. "It sure was," he said, confirming the prosecutor's guess. "It finished him off when he found out."

"You are plain crazy," the defense attorney moaned.

The prosecutor and judge gazed happily across the table at Traps, who was diligently peeling the rind from the Tête de Moine.

"Ah," the prosecutor asked, "how did the old

sinner find out? Did his juicy little piece of a wife admit to it?"

"She would never have done that, Prosecutor," Traps replied. "She was scared stiff of the old bastard."

"Did Gygax figure it out for himself?"

"Him? He was too conceited for that."

"Did you by any chance spring it on him, my dear friend and Don Juan?"

Involuntarily, Traps flushed. "Why, no, Kurt," he said. "What kind of guy do you think I am? It was one of his fine-feathered business friends who told the old crook."

"But why would he have done that?"

"He wanted to cook my goose. He was always out to get me."

"What types there are in this world!" the prosecutor exclaimed. "But how could this honest soul have known about your affair?"

"I told him."

"Told him?"

"Oh, well—over a glass of wine. You know how it is, you let things slip when you've had a drop too much."

"Granted." The prosecutor nodded agreement. "But you were just saying that you knew Gygax's business friend to be an enemy of yours. In that case, was it not fairly obvious to you that he would go to your boss with the story?"

At this point the defense attorney interceded. He rose to his feet, streaming perspiration, the collar of his frock coat soaked through. He would like to advise Traps, he declared, that he need not answer this question.

But Traps disagreed. "Why not?" he said. "There's no harm in the question. After all, I didn't give a damn whether Gygax found out or not. The way the old bastard had always treated me, the way he tried to give me the short end of the stick every time, I really didn't see any reason to be considerate of him."

For a moment another hush fell over the room, a deathly hush. Then a deafening tumult broke out, shouts of glee, a hurricane of laughter, a roar of jubilation. The taciturn, bald-headed man embraced Traps, even kissed him on both cheeks. The judge and the prosecutor danced around the room, staggered into the walls, shook hands with each other, clambered onto chairs, smashed bottles, reeled in a delirium of delight. "A second confession!" the prosecutor bellowed; he had scrambled up onto the arm of his chair and was now balancing on it, first on one leg and then the other. Hurrah for their guest—he was playing the game beautifully.

Even the defense attorney was doubled over with laughter. It was too rich, he exclaimed. One could not even be angry with such a defendant.

"The case is clear, the last link in the chain of evidence has been forged," the prosecutor continued, rocking on the chair like a weather-beaten baroque statue. "Behold our noble soul, our dearest Alfredo. We see him under the thumb of that stinker of a boss, and driving his secondhand Citroën about the country. Only a year ago, this was. He must nevertheless have taken pride in his position, our friend, the father of four children, the son of a factory hand. And rightly so. For during the war he had been a mere peddler; not even that, for he was unlicensed, a tramp going about with illegal textiles, a petty black-marketeer, traveling by railroad from village to village, or trudging on foot over dirt roads, making his weary way for miles through dark woods to remote farms, a dirty leather pouch slung over his shoulder, or possibly even a basket, and a battered suitcase in his hand. Now he had bettered himself, had found a foothold for himself in a good firm, was a member of the Liberal Party, whereas his father had been a crazy radical. But—if I may be permitted a poetic phrase—who rests upon the branch to which he has climbed when above his head stretch more branches bearing still finer fruit? Of course he was earning a good living, flitting about in his Citroën from place to place. The car wasn't bad, but our good Alfredo saw new models bobbing up all around him, roaring toward him, pulling up alongside him, passing him. Prosperity was spreading over the land. Why should he not have a piece of it?"

Traps beamed. "That's exactly how it was, Kurt. Exactly."

The prosecutor was in his element now, radiant, happy as a child on Christmas morning. "That was easier resolved than done," he continued, straddling the arm of his chair. "His boss would not let him rise in the world. Spitefully, crassly, openly, he exploited him, gave him advances only in order to impose new quotas, fettered him hand and foot, tied him down."

"Right you are!" the sales manager shouted

passionately. "You have no idea, gentlemen, how that old bastard put the squeeze on me."

"And so there was nothing for it but to go out for all you could get," the prosecutor said.

"Sure!" Traps agreed.

The defendant's interruptions inspired the prosecutor to further heights of eloquence. He stood up on his chair seat, waving his wine-spotted napkin like a banner, flaunting his vest sprinkled with bits of salad and meat and splashes of tomato sauce. "Our dear friend went at it first on the business level. Here, too, his conduct was not entirely ethical, as he himself admits. We can fairly well guess how he went about it. He secretly got in touch with his boss's suppliers, ferreted out what information he could, prom-ised better results, confused issues, talked with other salesmen, made alliances and counter-alli-ances. But then he hit on another way."

"Another way?" Traps asked in surprise.

The prosecutor nodded. "A way, gentlemen,

which led from the couch in Gygax's apartment directly into his marital bed."

All laughed, Traps even harder than the others. "Yes," he agreed, "it was a low-down trick I played on the old crook. But when I think back on it, the situation was just too funny. The fact is, I've always felt a little ashamed about it up to now. No one likes to go too deeply into his own actions, and, after all, nobody wears perfectly clean linen. But when I come up against such understanding friends as you, shame seems altogether out of place. It's odd, but I feel that you understand me, and I'm beginning to understand myself, as though I'm meeting a person who happens to be myself and whom I used to know only in a vague sort of way as a sales manager with a Studebaker and a wife and kids somewhere."

"We observe with pleasure," the prosecutor replied warmly, cordially, "that a light is dawning on our friend. Let us lend him our aid until

he sees it all in full lucidity. Let us track down
his motives with the merry zeal of archaeolo-
gists until we come upon the glory of buried
crimes. He began an affair with Frau Gygax.
How did this come about? Let us imagine that
he saw this juicy little piece one day. Perhaps
it was late one evening, possibly in winter—say,
around six o'clock."

Traps: "Around seven, Kurt, boy, around
seven!"

"With night already settled on the city, with
the street lamps shedding a golden glow, shop
windows and movie theaters all illuminated, and
green and yellow twinkling lights over the mar-
quees. It is the hour of cosy intimacy, of allure
and voluptuousness. He had driven his Citroën
up the slippery streets to the swanky residential
quarter where his boss lived—"

"Swanky residential quarter, that's exactly
it!" Traps interjected enthusiastically.

"A briefcase lay on the car seat beside him,

filled with orders, samples of cloth. An important decision had to be made, but Gygax's big limousine was not parked in its usual place at the curb. Nevertheless, he went up the path through the dark garden and rang the bell. Frau Gygax opened the door herself. Her husband would not be home tonight, she said, and her maid was out. She was dressed for an evening at home, or, better yet, was wearing a dressing gown. Nevertheless, Traps must come in for a drink; she invited him cordially, and so they sat together in the living room."

Traps was thunderstruck. "How do you know all this, Kurt, my boy? You're a wizard!"

"Practice," the prosecutor declared. "People's lives are all much the same. It was not even a case of seduction on Traps's part or the woman's; it was simply an opportunity that came his way. She was alone and bored, had nothing special in mind, was merely glad of the chance to talk with someone. The house was pleasantly warm, and under the flower-printed dressing gown she was wearing nothing but her night-gown. Traps, seated beside her, saw her white throat and the swell of her breasts, and as she talked in vindictive, disillusioned terms about her husband, the idea came to Traps that it was here he must apply his leverage—and in fact he had already begun by the time it occurred to him. He soon found out everything about Gygax—that the state of his health was shaky, that any disturbance might kill him. Traps learned his exact age, learned how coarse and crude he was with his wife, and how completely he took her faithfulness for granted. For you quickly find out everything from a woman who wants to take vengeance on her husband.

"And so our friend continued the affair, for now his plan was formed; now he was determined to ruin his boss by any and all means, come what might. And so the moment arrived when at last he held all the cards. He had won over the suppliers and Gygax's business partners, and at night he held naked in his arms the soft white body of the man's wife. And then he drew his noose tight; he produced a scandal. Deliberately. We can picture this last phase for ourselves. Again the intimate twilight hour. We find our friend in a restaurant, or, let us say, in one of those typical taverns of the old quarter of the city, somewhat overheated, the atmosphere in every way consonant with the spirit of our cantonal democracy, patriotic, solid, bull's-eye windows, everything substantial—the prices too, by the way. The bulky proprietor—"

"It was the Rathauskeller, old boy!" Traps exclaimed.

"Pardon, then, we must make a correction—the bulky proprietress sits surrounded by portraits of loyal customers of former years. A newspaper seller drifts through the place and goes out. Later, along comes a troupe from the Salvation Army, singing 'Let the sunshine in.' Some students are drinking with their professor. Traps at a table, two glasses, a bottle of good stuff in front of him—hang the expense right now. Opposite him, sallow, fat, drenched in sweat, collar open, as apoplectic a type as the intended victim, sits Gygax's business friend, wondering what this is all about, why Traps has invited him all of a sudden. He listens attentively, hears from Traps's own lips the admission of adultery. And then, a few hours later, as was inevitable, and as our Alfredo had foreseen, the fellow rushes off to the boss, convinced that duty, friendship, and decency demand that he let the unfortunate deceived husband know what he has learned."

"The hypocrite!" Traps cried. He listened with round, glistening eyes to the prosecutor's description, happy to be learning the truth, his own proud, courageous, unique truth.

The prosecutor continued: "Thus the fatal moment arrived, the moment so carefully calculated, when Gygax heard the whole story. The old crook was still able to drive home. Let us picture him filled with rage, perspiring profusely as he drives, stabbing pains in the region of his heart, hands shaking on the wheel, traffic policemen whistling angrily after him as he ignores signals. Then the laborious walk from the garage to the front door, collapse, perhaps in the hallway, as the little woman comes toward him, the juicy little piece. It does not take long; the doctor administers morphine, and then it is all over, finished—a brief rattling in the throat, and that is all, while the wife stands by the bed, sobbing. Traps, at home in the bosom of his family, lifts the telephone off the hook. Outward dismay, inner jubilation; the game is won. Hurrah! Three months later: the Studebaker."

This closing note evoked fresh gales of laughter. Traps, who had been batted from one amazement to the next, laughed along with the rest, although with a slight note of embarrassment. He scratched his head and gave the prosecutor an appreciative nod. He was in fine spirits. It had been a wonderfully successful evening. Of course, the fact that they imputed a murder to him upset him somewhat and made him a bit pensive. But he felt this mood as a pleasant one, for it awakened in him inklings of higher things, of justice, crime and punishment, guilt and atonement, and filled him with amazement at his own capacities. The fear, which he had not yet forgotten, that chill which had swept him in the garden and later during the hilarity at the table, now seemed to him utterly unfounded, part of the joke. It was all so human. He was eager to see what would follow.

The company moved into the parlor for their demitasse. Staggering, guiding the reeling attorney for the defense, Traps entered a room crammed with knickknacks and vases. There were enormous engravings on the wall, views of towns and historical subjects: the Rütli Oath, the victory of the Bernese over the Emperor's troops at the Battle of Laupen in 1339, the massacre of the Swiss Guard. The ceiling was stuccoed plaster; in one corner a grand piano; comfortable armchairs of huge dimensions, their antimacassars embroidered with pious sentiments: "Blessed be he who walks in the ways of righteousness"; "A clear conscience makes a soft pillow." Through the open window the highway could be sensed more than seen, magically present, a sunken path along which the headlights of cars came flaring only occasionally at this hour, for it was approaching two o'clock in the morning.

He had never heard anything as true-to-life as Kurt's account, Traps declared. There was scarcely anything to revise, as far as essentials went, although of course a few minor corrections were in order. For example, Gygax's kind-hearted business friend had been a shriveled little guy who wore a stiff collar not at all soaked with sweat. And Frau Gygax had received him not in a dressing gown, but in a kimono, and one so open that in all decency—if he might be permitted a little joke—he could not very well fail to open it the rest of the way. Also, the super-crook's well-deserved heart attack had struck him down at his warehouse, while the föhn was raging; the old bloke had not gone home, but had been taken to the hospital, where the heart had given out entirely. But, as he had said, these details were unimportant. The chief thing was that the theory of his bosom friend the prosecutor was correct: he had really become involved with Frau Gygax only because he wanted to ruin the old bastard. In fact, he remembered distinctly how, lying in Gygax's bed, on top of his wife, he had stared at the man's portrait photograph, which stood on the night table, had looked his fill at that fat, unpleasant face with its owl-like eyes behind horn-rimmed glasses, and how a kind of premonition had come over him, a wild, ecstatic delight at the thought that in what he was doing with such enjoyment and ardor he was really cutting the throat of his bastard of a boss, was cold-bloodedly finishing him off.

They were already seated in the soft chairs as Traps explained this, reaching out for the coffee, stirring it. With it they drank an 1893 cognac, Roffignac, out of big snifters.

It was time now to propose the sentence, the prosecutor announced. He sat sprawled athwart a monstrous reclining chair, his legs in their unmatched socks (one checked in gray and black, the other green) resting over the arm. "Our friend Alfredo did not act *dolo indirector*, and the ensuing death was not accidental. He is guilty *dolo malo*, of having acted with premeditation, as is clear from the facts that on the one hand he engineered the revelation and that

on the other hand after the super-crook's death
he ceased to visit the juicy little piece in question. Hence it necessarily follows that the
wife was only an instrument for his blood-
thirsty plans—the delectable murder weapon,
as it were. Clearly, then, we have a case of murder, performed by a psychological technique in
such a manner that, aside from adultery, nothing was done contrary to the law—to all ap-
pearances, at any rate. Wherefore, now that the
guise of innocence has vanished and our dear
defendant has been kind enough to make his
confession twice over, I have the pleasure as
prosecutor to demand that our high court impose the death penalty upon Alfredo Traps as
reward for a crime that merits admiration,
astonishment, and respect and may deservedly
be considered one of the most extraordinary
crimes of our century."

They laughed, applauded, and fell upon the

cake that Mlle Simone brought in. The crowning glory of the evening, they all declared.

Outside, as a special attraction, the late moon rose, a thin crescent. The trees rustled softly. Otherwise all was still; only rarely did a car pass on the road now. Occasionally there sounded the hesitant, uncertain footfalls of some belated homecomer. The sales manager felt secure, happy, sheltered. He sat beside Pilet on an overstuffed sofa whose antimacassar was embroidered with the words "East and west, home is best."

Pilet, still sparing of speech, said no more than an occasional "Splendid!" uttered with a heavily voiced, hissing S.

Traps pressed close to him with tender, affectionate familiarity, laid his cheek against Pilet's, admired his phlegmatic elegance. Sluggish and peaceful from the wine, he took a voluptuous pleasure in being himself in this understanding company, in no longer having a secret because secrecy was no longer necessary, in being appreciated, cherished, loved, understood. The idea that he had committed a murder became more and more acceptable to him; it touched him deeply, transformed his life, made everything more complex, more heroic, more precious. He was swept by a current of enthusiasm. He had planned and executed the murder, he told himself. He had done so in order to rise; but not so much to further his career, not so much for financial reasons, for the sake of owning a Studebaker. Rather, it was in order to become a more—what was the word?—a realer person, deeper, more worthy—he fumbled for the thought, having reached the limits of his intellect—more worthy of the respect and affection of educated, cultivated men who now seemed to him (even Pilet) like those ancient Magi whom he had once read about in the *Reader's Digest* and who had known not only the secrets of the stars, but the secrets of justice also. Justice—how the word intoxicated him! In his life as a salesman of textiles he had envisioned justice only as abstract pettifoggery; now it rose like a huge, incomprehensible sun over his limited horizon, an idea only vaguely grasped and for that reason all the more able to send shudders of awe through him. And so, sipping his cognac, he listened in profound astonishment at first and then with rising outrage to the arguments of his fat attorney for the defense, who zealously strove to fit his crime into the spheres of ordinary life, to reduce it to commonplace.

He had listened with pleasure to his esteemed opponent's ingenious oration, Herr Kummer began, lifting his pince-nez from the florid, swollen, shapeless lump of his nose and making his points with short, precise, geometrical gestures. Granted, the old crook Gygax was dead. Granted, his client had smarted under his dominion, had worked up a veritable animosity against the man, had tried to bring about his downfall. No one in his senses would deny this. And where, one might ask, where in the world of business did such things not occur? But it was utterly fantastic to represent as a murder the death of a businessman with a weak heart.

"But I did murder him!" Traps protested valiantly.

Unlike the prosecutor, Kummer declared, he considered the defendant not only innocent but even incapable of guilt.

Embittered, insulted, Traps interjected: "But I am guilty, I am."

"On the contrary," the lawyer continued, "our sales manager and sole agent for Hephaeston is one example among many. In declaring him incapable of guilt, I do not mean to assert that he is an innocent and stainless soul. Far from it. Traps has committed all the crimes of which he is capable; he has been guilty of adultery; he has swindled his way through life; he has shown a good deal of malignant spite. Not that his life has consisted only of adultery and swindling. Not at all, not at all. For it has had its positive sides; our friend Alfredo has his virtues. He is hard-working, hard-headed, loyal to his friends. He is trying to provide well for his children. He has sound political views. Taken all in all, we cannot detect more than an unethical taint, a slight spoilage, such as occurs and must occur in so many average lives. But for that very reason, on the other hand, he is not capable of a culpability that is great and pure and proud; he is not capable of a resolute deed, an unequivocal crime. He is not a criminal, but a victim of the age, of our Western civilization, which, alas, has fallen farther and farther away from Faith, from Christianity, from universals, succumbing more and more to the rule of chaos, so that the individual no longer may look up to a guiding star, and in place of order and true morality disorder and immorality reign, the law of the jungle prevails. Now, what has in truth taken place? This average man of ours, this man in the street, has fallen unforewarned into the hands of a crafty prosecutor who has probed, analyzed, dissected his purely instinctive management of his affairs in the textile industry; who has gone muckraking into his personal life and cast the harsh light of publicity upon the adventures of a man whose existence was compounded of business trips, the struggle for livelihood, and more or less innocent pleasures; a prosecutor who has tied together unrelated facts, forced a logical plan upon the disorganized whole, seized upon incidents that might as easily have taken quite another turn, and given them a casual significance; he has read intention where there was only accident, has twisted thoughtlessness into premeditation, so that in the end the interrogation could have no other outcome but to produce a murderer like a rabbit popping out of a magician's hat."

Traps: "That isn't so!"

"Let us regard the case of Gygax with sober objectivity, without being misled by the prosecutor's hocus-pocus. We can only conclude that the old crook had himself to thank for his death. His own irregular life destroyed his constitution. We all know only too well the familiar disease of the managerial personality. Its causes are restiveness, noise, a loveless marriage, strained nerves. As for the actual heart attack, the föhn that Traps mentioned is the crucial factor. The influence of the föhn upon cardiac patients is well known—"

"Ridiculous!" Traps exclaimed.

"In short Gygax's death was unquestionably a mere accident. Of course, I must admit that there was a certain ruthlessness in my client's behavior, but ruthlessness is obligatory under the normal laws of commercial life, as he himself repeatedly stressed. Of course he often felt a desire to kill his boss—after all, people will think anything, venture anything in thought, but only in thought, and that is precisely the point. It is absurd to assume that this thought was ever carried out in action, and even more absurd since my client has now been persuaded that he has actually committed a murder. The fact is that the breakdown of his automobile has been followed by a nervous breakdown, and therefore, as lawyer for the defense, I propose that Alfredo Traps be acquitted of this charge. . . ."

The sales manager was growing more and more indignant as he listened to the well-meaning fog in which his lovely crime was being shrouded, distorted, dissolved, rendered unreal and shadowy, a product of the state of the atmosphere. He felt belittled, and flared up violently almost as soon as his lawyer completed the defense. Rising outraged to his feet, a plate with a fresh piece of cake balanced in his right hand, his glass of Roffignac in his left, he declared that before sentence was pronounced he wanted to insist with the utmost firmness that he agreed wholeheartedly with the prosecutor's speech. Tears filled his eyes. It had been a murder, a deliberate, premeditated murder, he said. He understood that now, and had been profoundly disappointed—horrified, in fact—by the lawyer's defense. He had thought that if anyone would understand him, he could count on understanding from this friend. And so now he demanded the verdict, or rather the sentence, not out of any groveling desire to please, but out of pure idealism, for only in the course of this wonderful night had it dawned on him what it meant to lead a true life, to be true to oneself (at this point our good, honest Traps grew somewhat muddled), for to the true life, sublimer ideas of justice, of punishment fitting the crime, were as essential as the chemical elements and compounds that made up his synthetic textile, to stick to the field he was at home in. This was a revelation that had resulted in a new birth for him. At any rate—he hoped they would make allowances for the fact that his vocabulary was rather limited outside his own field, so that he found it hard to express what he really meant—at any rate, rebirth seemed to him the proper word for the overwhelming and glorious joy that was now sweeping through him like a typhoon, turning everything upside down inside him, making a new man of him.

And so there was nothing left but the verdict. Amid the howls of screeching laughter and attempts at yodeling by Pilet, the tiny judge, by now drunk as a lord, announced his decision. It was a matter of some difficulty, not only because he had clambered onto—or, rather, into—the opened grand piano in the corner, but also because his tongue tripped repeatedly. He stumbled over his words, twisted and mutilated them, started sentences he could not finish, continued others whose purport he had already forgotten. But the general sense of it could be guessed. The question at issue was, he declared, whether the prosecutor or the attorney for the defense was right; whether Traps had committed the most extraordinary crime of the century or was innocent as a lamb. He, the judge, found himself unable to subscribe completely to either view. As the attorney for the defense maintained, Traps had been tricked and trapped by the prosecutor's examination, and consequently had admitted to a good many things that had not happened precisely in the way described. But, on the other hand, he had committed murder, though not out of diabolic premeditation, rather by sharing in the ethical indifference of the world in which he functioned as sales manager for a synthetic textile named Hephaeston. He had killed because it was utterly natural for him to drive another man to the wall, to proceed ruthlessly, come what might. In the world through which he roared at high speed in his Studebaker, there would have been no serious consequences for their dear Alfredo; but now he had had the kindness to come here to them, to their quiet little house among the trees (at this point the judge's exposition became rather nebulous, and he brought out the rest of his argument to the accompaniment of joyful sobs, interrupted now and again by a tremendous sneeze of deep emotion, his little head disappearing behind an enormous handkerchief, while the others roared louder and louder with laughter) —to their quiet, white-painted, cozy little home, to four old men who had illumined his world with the pure radiance of justice, which, to be sure, often bore strange features, he knew, knew, knew very well that the justice grinning out of four weather-beaten faces, reflected in the monocle of a white-haired prosecutor and the pince-nez of an obese attorney for the defense, sniggering out of the toothless mouth of a drunken judge who could barely control his tongue and gleaming with a red glow upon the bald pate of an executioner emeritus (growing impatient over this lapse into poetry, the others howled: "The verdict, the verdict!")—this justice was indeed a grotesque, crotchety, pensioned-off justice, but as such it was still and nevertheless and in spite of everything *justice* ("The verdict, the verdict!"), in whose name he now sentenced their dearest, their best, their noblest Alfredo to death. . .

The lawyer, the prosecutor, the executioner, and Mlle Simone shouted huzzahs, and Traps, now sobbing with emotion, cried: "Thank you, dear Judge, thank you!"

. . . although the sole real judicial basis for this verdict was the condemned man's own admission of guilt. But, after all, was not that the most important factor?

"I therefore take pleasure in delivering a verdict that the condemned man approves without qualification. Mercy would be incompatible with the dignity of man, and our honored friend and

guest may now joyfully receive the crowning
glory of his murder in circumstances that, I
may hope, he will regard with no less satis-
faction than the murder itself. The fatality that
comes to the average man, to the man in the
street, as chance will have it, in the form of
an automobile accident, or as a mere imposition of nature, disease, the obstruction of a
blood vessel by an embolism, a malignant
growth, here emerges as the moral and indispensable outcome; in our sentence, life is per-
fected with logical consistency, like a work
of art, and the human tragedy is revealed in
all its beauty, shines radiantly, is welded into
flawless form. . . ."

"Finish, finish!" the others shouted.

"Indeed, I need not hesitate to declare that
only the act of judgment which transforms
the defendant into a condemned man truly
confers the accolade of justice. There can be
nothing nobler, nothing greater, nothing more

sublime than the condemnation of a man to death. Therefore I now pronounce this sentence. Traps—who perhaps does not entirely deserve his luck, as, strictly speaking, a straightforward verdict of premeditated homicide is not altogether justified—but I will not in any way commute the sentence, for I would not wish to disappoint our dear friend—in short, Alfredo is now one of us, a peer, worthy to be taken into our company and recognized as a master player of the game. . . ."

The others roared him down. "Bring on the champagne!"

The evening had reached its climax. The champagne bubbled; there was no cloud upon their merriment; even the attorney for the defense was taken fraternally to their hearts. The candles had burned down; some had already glimmered out. The first hint of dawn wavered outside the windows; the stars were fading and the air carried a suggestion of cool dew and distant sunrise.

Traps was still soaring with exaltation, but also tired out; he asked to be led to his room, and staggered into the arms of each of his friends in turn. All babbled drunkenly, monologues, meaningless speeches; an enormous roar of voices filled the room, for no one was listening to anyone else. Reeking of wine and odorous of cheese, they patted the sales manager's head, caressed him, kissed him. Happy, exhausted, he submitted to their caresses like a child among a group of grandfathers and uncles.

At last the taciturn, bald-headed man led Traps upstairs. It was a toilsome ascent on all fours; halfway up they could go no further and sprawled on the steps, arms and legs entangled. From a window above a stony dawn light fell upon the whiteness of the plaster walls. From outside came the first noises of a new day—the distant whistling at tiny railroad stations, sounds of shunting, vague reminders of a missed opportunity to return home.

Traps was in seventh heaven, all his desires satiated as they had never been before in his uneventful life. Dim images floated through his mind: the face of a boy, probably his youngest, who was his favorite child; then, mistily, the village in which he had landed as the result of his breakdown; the bright ribbon of the road swinging over a small rise; the hillock on which the church sat; the great rustling oak with the iron rings and props; the wooded hills; the glowing, infinite sky beyond, above, all around.

But then the bald man collapsed. "Want to sleep, want to sleep, tired, tired," he murmured, and forthwith dozed off while Traps crawled on up the stairs. The bald man remained conscious just long enough to hear a chair fall over. For brief seconds the noise awoke him out of his dreams and memories of dread duties long gone by. Then a tangle of legs passed over the sleeping man as the others climbed the steps. Croaking and squeaking, the others had scribbled out a death sentence on parchment, choicely worded, filled with witty turns of phrase, with archaic language and academic tags in Latin. Then they had started up to lay the product of their wit upon the bed of the sleeping sales manager, so that when he awoke he would find a pleasant memento of their tremendous drinking bout.

Outside the brightness grew. Birds began crying harshly and impatiently. And so they stormed up the stairs, clambering over the bald-headed man in his sleep of innocence. Clutching one another, each supporting the next, all three staggering, pushing, pulling, and crawling, interfering with one another on the landing, so that retreat and a new start were necessary, they arrived at last at the door to the guestroom. The judge opened it—and then the solemn group, the prosecutor still with the napkin tied around his neck, froze to immobility.

In the window frame hung Traps, motionless, a dark silhouette against the dull silver of the sky, amid the heavy fragrance of roses floating in through the open window—hung so definitely and so finally that the prosecutor, from whose monocle the gathering morning light was reflected with a brightness that increased by the second, had to gasp for air before, in perplexed helplessness and sadness over the loss of his friend, he cried, grief-stricken: "Alfredo, my good Alfredo! For God's sake, what were you thinking of? You've ruined the most wonderful evening we've ever had!"

A note about the Author

FRIEDRICH DUERRENMATT is the son of a Protestant minister, and the grandson of a poet. He was born in Konolfingen, Switzerland, and studied theology, philosophy, and literature at the universities of Zurich and Bern. In 1947 he began to write—short prose, thrillers, literary criticism, and movie, radio, and television scripts. Five years later *Fools are Passing Through*, a comedy (produced off-Broadway in 1958), carried his name beyond the frontiers of German-speaking countries. Today Duerrenmatt's plays—including, of course, his fabulously successful *The Visit*—are produced on Broadway, as well as throughout Europe, in Japan, and in South America. In 1959 he was awarded the New York Critics Award for the best foreign play. His stories have been translated into most European languages. His novels published in this country—THE JUDGE AND HIS HANGMAN, THE PLEDGE, and THE QUARRY—have established his fame as a great teller of tales.

Married to a Swiss actress, Herr Duerrenmatt, the father of three children, lives near Neuchâtel in an old peasant house overlooking the lake.

THREE IMPORTANT NOVELISTS
NOW PUBLISHED BY BALLANTINE BOOKS

THOMAS BERGER

Author of the current best-seller, **Little Big Man,** a major event in American fiction. Now in print as a Ballantine paperback: **Crazy in Berlin,** Berger's famous first novel. Coming soon: **Reinhart in Love.**

U6014   CRAZY IN BERLIN   75¢

ANTHONY BURGESS

Acclaimed by reviewers as "the ablest satirist to appear since Evelyn Waugh." Author of **Nothing Like the Sun** and **The Clockwork Orange.** Two novels now in print in Ballantine editions:

U5030   THE WANTING SEED   60¢
U5031   HONEY FOR THE BEARS   60¢

NIKOS KAZANTZAKIS

The greatest Greek writer of the Twentieth Century, author of **The Odyssey: A Modern Sequel, The Greek Passion,** and **Zorba The Greek,** now a major motion picture. Ballantine editions now in print:

U6020   ZORBA THE GREEK   75¢
U7027   FREEDOM OR DEATH   95¢

For a complete catalog of Ballantine Books, write in care of Dept. C. S., Ballantine Books, Inc., 101 Fifth Avenue, New York, New York 10003.

BALLANTINE HISTORICAL NOVELS

IMMORTAL QUEEN, by Elizabeth Byrd

A novel of Mary, Queen of Scots. "A full-bodied, eye-riveting historical. Put it on the same shelf with GONE WITH THE WIND and Anya Seton's KATHERINE."

—Chicago Tribune

U 7010   640 pages   95¢

BY VALOUR AND ARMS, by James Street

A novel of Vicksburg in the Civil War, by the author of TAP ROOTS. "Maintains all the high standards set by this novelist in past work. Incident, action, and characters speed toward the climax with the inexorable logic of a Mississippi flood."

—Boston Globe

U 7016   560 pages   95¢

THE GROVE OF EAGLES, by Winston Graham

A blazing novel of Elizabethan England in the time of the Second Spanish Armada. "Masterly story-telling, swaggering adventure . . . one of the most deservedly popular novels of the year."

Orville Prescott, *New York Times*

U 7020   576 pages   95¢

THE CORNERSTONE, by Zoe Oldenbourg

A towering novel of medieval France, winner of the *Prix Femina* and a Book-of-the-Month Club choice. "Without question one of the great historical novels of our time."

Harrison Smith, *Saturday Review*

U 7030   576 pages   95¢

To order by mail, send 95¢ plus 5¢ for postage and handling to: Dept. CS, Ballantine Books, Inc., 101 Fifth Avenue, New York, N. Y. 10003

LOVE, WAR AND FANCY

The unexpurgated text of Sir Richard Burton's famous account of the sexual customs of the East

---

Sir Richard Burton, translator of *The Kama Sutra* and *The Persian Garden*, was a lifelong enemy of prudery and the foremost authority of his century on the sexual customs of the East.

LOVE, WAR AND FANCY, edited by the eminent British sexologist, Kenneth Walker, is the summation of his writings on the sexual *mores* of the Arabs. It consists of Burton's famous "Terminal Essay" to the privately printed 12-volume edition of *The Arabian Nights*, together with his notes on Arabian manners and psychology. To those who know *The Arabian Nights* only in the bowdlerized version published in the United States, LOVE, WAR AND FANCY will come as a revelation.

U 6016   288 pages   75¢

To order by mail, send 75¢ plus 5¢ for postage and handling to: Dept. CS, Ballantine Books, 101 Fifth Avenue, New York, N. Y. 10003.

AND DON'T MISS THESE RECENT TITLES
FROM BALLANTINE BOOKS